W9-BMC-576

HERGÉ

★

THE ADVENTURES OF

TINTIN

★

THE CRAB WITH THE GOLDEN CLAWS

LITTLE, BROWN AND COMPANY
New York Boston

Artwork © 1953 by Casterman, Paris and Tournai.
Library of Congress Catalogue Card Number Afo 13927
Copyright © renewed 1981 by Casterman
Library of Congress Catalogue Card Number R 104021
Translation Text © 1958 Egmont UK Ltd.
Translated by Leslie Lonsdale-Cooper and Michael Turner
American Edition © 1974 by Little, Brown and Company (Inc.), N.Y.

All rights reserved. Except as permitted under the U.S. Copyright Act of 1976, no part of this publication may be reproduced, distributed, or transmitted in any form or by any means, or stored in a database or retrieval system, without the prior written permission of the publisher.

Little, Brown and Company

Hachette Book Group
237 Park Avenue, New York, NY 10017
Visit our website at www.lb-kids.com

Little, Brown and Company is a division of
Hachette Book Group, Inc.
The Little, Brown name and logo are trademarks of
Hachette Book Group, Inc.

The publisher is not responsible for websites (or their content) that are not owned by the publisher.

First Paperback Edition: June 1974

Library of Congress catalog card no. 73-21249
ISBN: 978-0-316-35833-0
30 29 28
Published pursuant to agreement with Casterman, Paris
Not for sale in the British Commonwealth
Printed in China

THE CRAB WITH THE GOLDEN CLAWS

?

Yow! . . . ow! . . . ow!

?

There you are, Snowy. You see what comes of your dirty habit of exploring rubbish bins . . . I don't go scavenging, do I?

You've been lucky! You could have cut yourself. Look how jagged the edges are.

Now, come on! . . . And don't do that again, or I'll buy a muzzle and you'll walk on a lead!

Hi! Hello there, Tintin!

OLYMPIA BA

Waiter, bring another drink!
Yes, sir.

My dear Tintin, how nice to see you again! . . .

To be precise: how nice to see you again, my dear Tintin!

Here you are, sir.

Your health!
And yours!

My dear old friends, how nice to see you again!

Well, now, what's going on?

Everything's fine: we've just been entrusted with a very important case.
Oh?. . .

To be precise: a very . . . er . . . important case.
Oh?. . .

Look . . . Have you read this?
"Watch out for counterfeit coins!" . . . Yes, I saw it.

Well, we two have been instructed to clear this thing up.
Oh?. . . Jolly good!. . . I say, is it easy to spot one of these fakes?

Oh, you know how it is. People like ourselves who have examined them can tell one in a flash, of course . . .

Waiter! . . . How much?

Forty-five pence, sir.
Here's fifty pence! . . . But most people are easily fooled by them.

I'm sorry, sir . . .
Good gracious, someone's slipped me a dud fifty-pence piece!
CLUNK

There!
Thank you.

If you've nothing better to do, come along with us. We'll show you the papers we've already collected in our investigations.
Thanks.

Where did you put those papers?
But you put them away yourself!

!

What's that?
That? . . . It all came from Police Headquarters. They are things taken from a body found in the sea. Did you notice? He had five coins on him, all duds . . . Odd, don't you think?

Very odd! . . . May I . . . ?

I'll be back in a minute!
?
?

I'm going after him!

What's bitten him!

Good gracious! I've forgotten my stick!

Good gracious! He's forgotten his stick!

There he is!
We've caught him up.

What on earth's the matter? . . .
Well, the scrap of paper among those things found on the drowned man comes from the label off a tin . . .

. . . and I was holding the very tin from which it was torn, just before I met you! Here we are. I threw it into that dustbin . . . that one where the tramp is rummaging.

Tintin! . . . Aren't you ashamed of yourself? Rummaging in dustbins like a common mongrel off the streets!
One moment, please . . .

It's gone! . . . Yet I'm sure I threw it there. A tin of crab, I remember quite clearly.

Open your sack!

No, it's not here . . .
!

That's odd; in fact, it's fishy.
To be precise: it's fishy . . .

What's all the fuss about?
Those chaps are absolutely daft! They are looking for an empty tin! A crab tin . . .

A crab tin! Are they indeed!

Now, let's have a good look at this bit of paper . . .

Aha! That's interesting! There's something written here in pencil, almost obliterated by the water . . .

I must look at this through a magnifying glass.

!

Gnawing a bone again? Where did this one come from? . . .

Can't you ever do as you're told?

There! . . . And mind you don't do it again!

? ? ?

Did I leave it in my study? . . .

It's not here either!

CRASH
?

Crumbs! That made me jump . . . And it was only the wind slamming the door!

But now I think of it, that bit of paper . . .

. . . must have been blown away when I went into my study the first time to get my magnifying glass!

That's the answer. There it is!

Now let's have a look . . .

Have I gone crazy? I'm positive I put my magnifying glass down here a moment ago!

?

I'll go over all this in pencil. There's 'K' . . . and an 'A' . . . and that's an 'R' . . . or an 'I' . . . there, I'll soon have it . . .

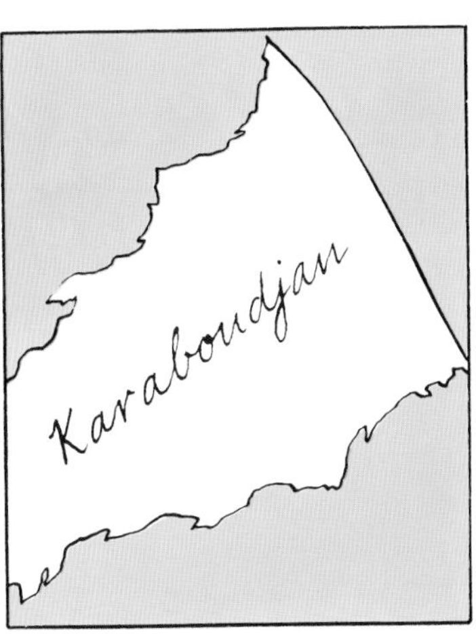
Karaboudjan

KARABOUDJAN . . . that's an Armenian name. Karaboudjan . . .

An Armenian name. So . . . now what? . . . That doesn't help me much!

HELP!
HELP!

What's going on? . . .

That was my landlady's voice. I must go and see what's happened.

It was a Japanese or a Chinese gentleman with a letter for you, Mr Tintin. But just as he was going to give it to me a car came by, and stopped . . .

. . . outside the door. Three men got out; they attacked the Chinese gentleman and knocked him down! . . . Of course I shouted: 'Help! Help!' but one of the gangsters threatened me with a huge revolver, as big as that! Then they threw the Japanese gentleman into their car and drove off . . . with the letter addressed to you . . .

A tin + a drowned man + five counterfeit coins + Karaboudjan + a Japanese + a letter + a kidnapping = a real Chinese puzzle.

The next morning . . .
RRRING
RRRING
RRRING

Hello? . . . Yes . . . Oh, it's you! . . . What's the news? . . . What? . . .

Yes, the drowned man has been identified: the one who had the mysterious bit of paper and the five dud coins. His name was Herbert Dawes: he was a sailor from the merchant-ship KARABOUDJAN.

The merchant-ship KARABOUDJAN! Did you say KARABOUDJAN? . . .

To the docks, Snowy . . . as quick as we can!

KARABOUDJAN
79

KARABO

What a lot of seagulls!

WHAT THE . . . ?!

341

Confound it! . . . Missed him!

Well, Snowy my lad, if I hadn't happened to be watching the seagulls we'd have been flattened . . .
540

What happened? . . .
Oh, it's you! Well, I just missed being squashed by that heavy crate! . . . But what are you doing here?
The chain broke . . .

We are going aboard the KARABOUDJAN to inquire about the sailor who was drowned.
Are you? May I come too? It would give me a chance to look round the ship . . .

Will you be long on board?
No, only about half an hour.

He's coming aboard with the two detectives!

You take care of him, while I talk to them . . . He mustn't go back on shore!
I get it!

All right then? . . . I'll wait for you here in half an hour . . .
Here? . . . Good.

How do you do, Mister Mate. We've come about that unfortunate sailor . . .
I'm at your service, gentlemen. Will you come into my cabin? We can talk more easily there . . .

Mind the step . . .
Yes, I see it.

. . . and the door is a bit low . . .

. . . so this sailor used to drink. On the night of his death you met him in the town, very drunk; then he fell into the water trying to get back to the ship. Plain as a pikestaff!
To be precise: plain as a pikestaff.
OLD SCOTCH WHISKY
HABANA

Excuse me, Mister Mate. I just wanted to tell you I've finished that job.
Good, I'll come and see.

As a matter of fact, we must go too. We have already taken up too much of your time.
Not at all! I'm delighted to have been able to help.

Yes, that door really is a little low . . .
A little low, yes . . .
A little too low . . .

The young man who came aboard with you asked me to say that he couldn't wait: he's just gone.
Oh! Tintin! . . . We'd quite forgotten him . . .

Mind the step.
Goodbye!
Goodbye!

What can have happened to Tintin?

They've put me in the bottom of the hold, the brutes! I wonder . . . Ah! someone's coming.

Are you keeping up this little joke for long?
Yes and no, my young friend. It all depends . . .

At least tell me why I'm tied up here in the hold . . .
It's no use pretending. You know why better than we do.

But . . .
SLAM

Snowy! ! Good old Snowy! How did you get in here? . . . It must have been while those two scoundrels . . .

Ssh! . . . Listen . . .

TOOOOOT

We're sailing . . . for an unknown destination. But it's no good rotting away down here. Snowy, bite through these ropes and we'll take the first chance we get to say goodbye to these pirates!

Here's a coded radio message just in from the Boss. Read it . . .
'Send T to the bottom'

And I've just sent Pedro down with some food for him! . . . Oh well! I'll take a rope and a lump of lead, and that'll soon fix him.

It's very kind of you to bring me that, but how am I going to eat with my hands tied behind my back?

You're right, I'll have to loosen them a bit. But mind you, no tricks . . .

. . . make one false move . . . you get me? . . .

?

. . . he asked me to free his hands so he could eat; but as soon as I bent down he hit me a terrific crack . . .
. . . and that's nothing to what the mate will do to you!

Idiot! . . . Nitwit! . . . Now we'll have to find him, you fool!
. . . and now he's got a gun.

I hope these are cases of food. Then we can withstand a siege behind our barricade! Anyway . . .
TOP
FRAGILE
BOTTOM
TOP
FRAGILE
BOTTOM

Let's see . . .

Great snakes! . . . Tins of crab!

No doubt about it, these are the same as the tin we tried to find! . . .

We'll sort that out later. Let's go on checking our stores.

Champagne too! Snowy my boy, our supplies are taken care of!
And how!

Let me offer you a drink, Snowy . . .

Ssh! . . .

Quiet! . . . They're looking for us! They mustn't find us . . .

BANG

It's no good trying to open that door. He'll have barricaded himself in. We'll starve him out: he's nothing to eat . . .

. . . that's what you think, gentlemen!

!?

Opium! . . .

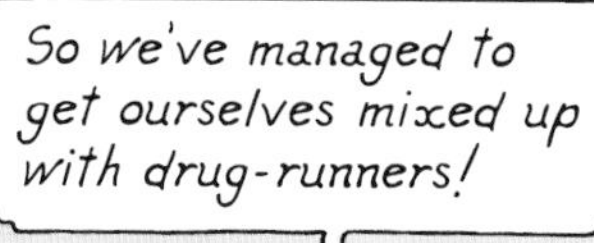
So we've managed to get ourselves mixed up with drug-runners!

This certainly changes everything! They were quite right: we've nothing to eat! . . .
Who cares? We've plenty to drink!

Let's see if we can't get out somehow.
Golly, how she rolls!

No, we can't reach the port-hole above; it's too far . . .

Unless . . . yes, I've got an idea . . .

Meanwhile . . .

Mister Mate, the Captain wants you . . .
The Captain? . . . What does he want, the old drunkard?

Yes, I sent f-f-for you, Mister Mate; it's wicked! I'm . . . it's wicked! . . . I'm being allowed to d-die of thirst! . . . I . . . I haven't a d-d-drop of whisky!
That's quite intolerable, Captain. I'll have some sent in at once.

At any rate, you-you-you are my friend, Mr Allan. You're the only one who . . . one who . . . who . . .
Of course, of course, you know I wouldn't deprive you of whisky for anything in the world . . .

For then I'll be the boss on this ship and do just as I like!

That night . . .

Now it's dark I'll try out my plan.

BONK
?

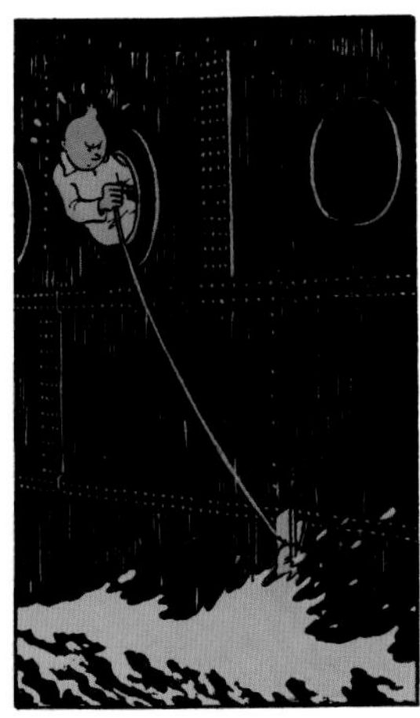

Let's have another shot.

No one there! But what . . . ?
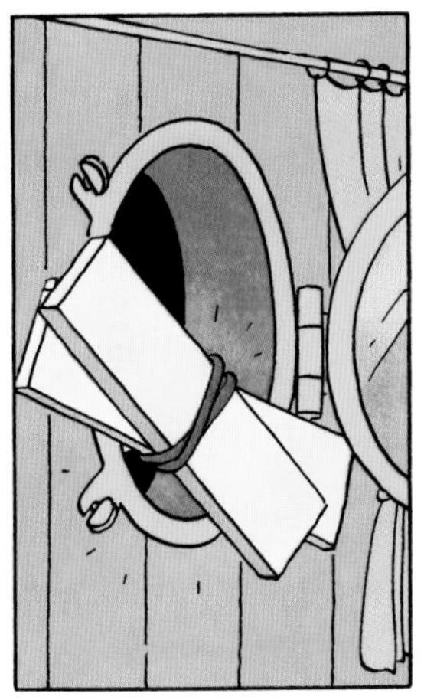

. . . perhaps it's the whisky . . .

OLD WHISKY

Ssh! . . . Not a sound!
Who-who . . . who are you?

Someone forced to sail in this vile tub and . . .
Vile tub? . . . I . . . d-d-do you know I'm Captain Haddock! And I can have you -y-y-you clapped in irons!

Thanks! I've just got out of them! I've spent enough time in your hold with its cargo of opium!
O-o-opium? There's opium in the hold? . . . In my hold . . . m-m-mine? . . .

Didn't you know?
Opium! . . . But h-h-how? . . . It's frightful! . . . I'm an hon . . . an honest man . . . and not . . . but who . . . ? It must be Allan, the f-first mate, who has . . . he . . . he's double-crossing me . . .

Listen, you must help me. And you must promise to stop drinking. Think of your reputation, Captain! What would your old mother say if she saw you in such a state? . . .
M-m-my old mother? . . .

There, there, Captain! . . .
Boo hoo . . . Boo . . . hoo . . . hoo Booh . . . hoo Booh . . . hoo.

For goodness' sake be quiet . . .
Boo . . . hoo . . . Mummy! M-M-Mummy!

Let's go and see. Perhaps he's gone crazy . . .

Too late! I'm trapped . . .
Mummy . . . Boo . . . hoo . . . hoo . . .

What's going on here? . . .
Mummy . . . Boo . . . hoo . . . hoo . . .

I'm a miserable wretch . . .
Here, drink this . . . You'll feel better . . .

FFFFH

N-n-no . . . I . . . I promised him not to drink . . . and I won't any more!
Who did you promise that to? . . .

To the y-y-young man who . . . who who . . . who was here . . .
What young man? Answer me!

By thunder!
I don't know . . . I've never seen him before.

The little devil! So he managed to get in here! . . . Luckily that drunken bawling scared him off. But he may try to come back . . .

Jumbo, stay and watch this port-hole. If anyone tries to climb in here, get him. Understand? . . . here's a gun . . .
Right.

We must settle his hash! We'll blow in the door of the hold where he's hiding!

That's it! . . . Take cover . . .

BOOM

That must have knocked him out . . .
Or else he's shamming . . .

The swine!
BANG

BANG
BANG
BANG

A champagne cork!
In that case . . .

BANG

?
BANG

Quick! Back again! . . .

?!?

I watched the port-hole carefully, Mister Mate, but not the locker under the bunk . . . And that's where he was hiding! . . .

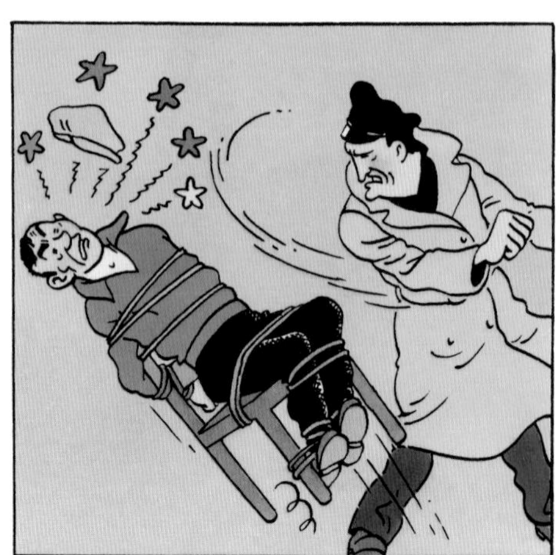

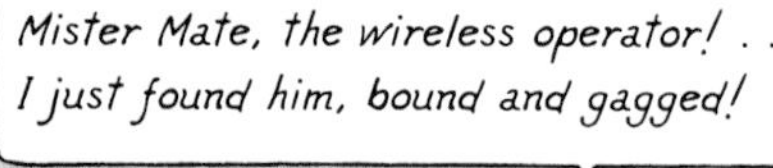
Mister Mate, the wireless operator! . . . I just found him, bound and gagged!

!!

It's a rum thing, Mister Mate! . . . The longboat has vanished!

Dawn at last. We're safe for the moment: the KARABOUDJAN has disappeared over the horizon.

But we're not out of trouble yet! We must be sixty miles from the Spanish coast. We must save our energy. You sleep for a bit. Then I'll have a rest while you take a turn at the oars.
OK.

Heavens, I'm thirsty! . . . And cold! . . .

I remember: there's a keg of fresh water here, and biscuits . . .

. . . and some rum!

But I swore never to drink again, and I'll keep my word!

Maybe if I only had a little drop . . .

. . . just to warm myself up?

Aaaah! . . . the stuff the cold
That's to keep out!

Now, just one more sip . . .

and I'll throw it away . . .

Hello, it's empty already!

Poor l-l-little chap! He's fast asleep!

But he must be f-f-frightfully c-c-cold, too . . .

Aha! I've got an idea . . .

!?

Our oars! Hey! . . .
You're burning our oars!
Have you gone mad? . . .

Ah! here's
a bucket!

If . . . if you p-p-put that out . . .
y-you'll have to settle with m-m-me,
you miserable whipper-snapper . . .

Let go of that bucket, you
meddlesome cabin-boy!
?

?

What have I done? Oh, Columbus
. . . What have I done!
You've got us into a fine
mess . . .

I'm sorry . . . I'm sorry! . . . I'm a
miserable wretch . . . I drank the
rum from the locker . . . I'm
sorry! . . .
Ssh! . . .

A seaplane! . . .
We're saved! . . .

It's got Moroccan
markings: CN.

CN-3411
RAT
TAT
TAT
TAT
TAT
TAT
TAT

Beasts! . . . Swine! . . . Cowards! . . .
Look out! He's coming back!

RAT TAT
RAT TAT TAT
TAT

Hooray! . . . Splendid! . . . Bang in the middle!
PFTT
PFTT
Well, at least I hit him!

The engine's stopped . . .
Look, they're getting out.

Just our luck! . . . A single bullet, and it has to go and cut the main ignition lead! But it won't take long to mend.
You do it. I'll keep an eye on them . . .
CN

Look, they're both on the same side. I'll dive: swim underwater as far as I can, beyond them, and when I come up I should be out of their sight, and near the plane.
You can't possibly . . .

Getting on?
Yes, it's nearly done.

CN-3411

Finished?
That's it! . . . I'll just fix the last bolt.
CN

CN
!
Hands up!

Get back . . . and no tricks! I'm a good shot!

He's done it! . . . What a boy! . . .

Good. Try and find some rope to tie up these two toughs.
CN

Tie them up? Why? . . . Let's just pitch them into the sea! They didn't worry about shooting us up, the gangsters!
I know, but we aren't gangsters! . . . Come on, Captain, tie them up and let's get going.

Now then: who hired you two for this shady business?
So! I see why you pretended to be so big-hearted! You wanted to pump us! Well, we aren't talking! . . .

As you like. But perhaps you'll find your tongues when the police get their hands on you.
Hey, can you fly an aeroplane? . . .

CN34

You're sure this is the right direction for Spain? . . .
Er . . . yes . . . but it remains to be seen if we'll get there. We're in for a rough time.

Oh, Columbus, this is frightful! . . . We'll never come through alive!

Oho, a bottle! . . . Now if only it were whisky . . .

And it is whisky! . . .

Since we've got to die, I may as well have one last bottle . . .

Hey, it looks f-f-fun doing that . . . L-l-let me have a go!
This is hardly the moment . . .

B-b-but I w-w-want to! . . .
Leave that alone! . . .

Whew, what luck! . . . I just managed to right her . . .

Quick, look behind you!
N-n-now then you whippersnapper! I don't c-c-care for your tricks! . . .
No good, he can't hear above the engine.

W-w-will y-you let me t-take over: yes or no? . . . One . . . two . . . three . . .
Leave me alone!

Then take that, you pig-headed . . .

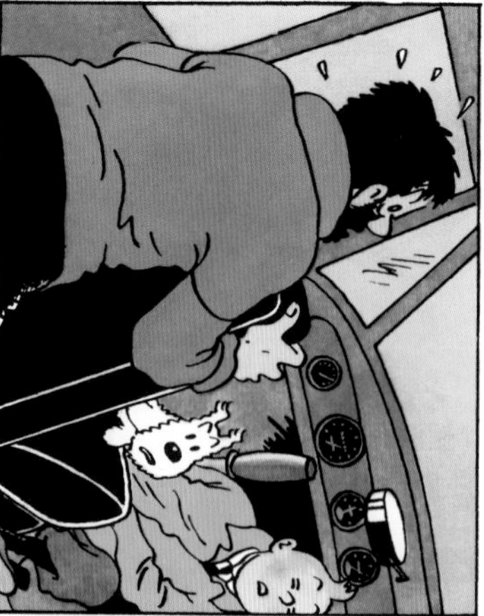

Great snakes! What happened?

Help! . . . We're going to crash . . .

CN-34|11

CN-34|11

That was a near thing!

Good heavens! . . . The two prisoners? . . . They're still in the plane . . .

Stop! . . . You're crazy! . . .
CN-34

CN-3

Poor Tintin! . . . He's finished . . .
CN-34

Here . . . take this one! . . .
I'll get the other . . .

Well, here we are! . . . Do you really think this looks like Spain?
Er . . . I . . . anyway it should be . . .

Wooah! Wooah! Wooah!

?

What a bone! . . . Where on earth did you find it?

Come and see! . . . There are lots more . . .

?
!
See? . . . Bones for everybody . . .

A camel! . . .
A camel? . . . But there aren't any camels in Spain . . .

Unfortunately we aren't in Spain! . . . We're in the middle of the Sahara Desert!
In the middle of the Sahara! . . . then that animal . . . that animal . . . that animal died of . . . died of . . .

. . . died of thirst, of course!

What's the matter? . . . Feeling faint?
The land of thirst! . . . The land of thirst! . . .

The land of thirst . . .
Courage, Captain, courage! We aren't finished yet.
It looks as if he's at the end of his tether.

The land of thirst . . .
The prisoners have gone!

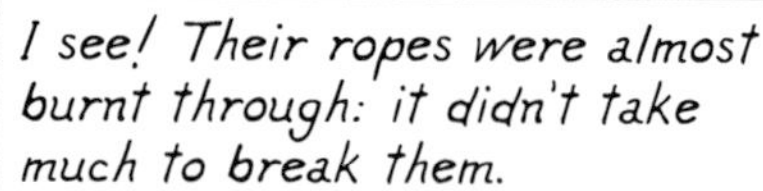
I see! Their ropes were almost burnt through: it didn't take much to break them.

The land of thirst . . .

Look over there . . . they're too far away now for us to catch them up. Never mind . . .

Come on, Captain! Perhaps we shall be lucky and come across a well!
The land of thirst . . .

A drink! . . . A drink! . . . I can't go on . . .
Courage, Captain! We'll rest a bit in the shadow of the sand- dune . . .

There, lie down for a while: it'll do you good.

Tintin . . . where are you? . . . A drink! . . .

Just an empty horizon . . . Nothing but endless desert . . .
A drink! . . .

?!?

I wonder how we can get out of this.

A bottle of champagne! I'll open it!

This confounded cork. It won't come out! . . .
You brute: Take that!

Golly, what have I done?? . . .

Thanks all the same, Snowy . . .
I did my best.
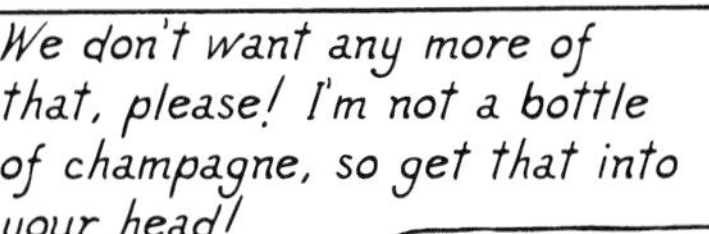
We don't want any more of that, please! I'm not a bottle of champagne, so get that into your head!

A drink! . . .

?
Look! . . . A lake! . . . Water! . . . Water! . . .

Stop! Stop! . . . It's a mirage! . . .
Water! . . . Water! . . .

Didn't I tell you it was a mirage? There isn't a lake.
But I saw it . . .

Some hours later . . .

Aha! . . . There's a bottle of wine!
Where can he see a bottle?

I'll uncork it . . .
? ? !

I hear you call help?
?!?!

Whew! What a ghastly nightmare!

Where am I? . . . What happened? . . .
You come with me to Lieutenant.

He come, sir . . . the young boy.
Ah! there you are. Come in! I'm glad to see you on your feet again.

I'm Lieutenant Delcourt, in command of the outpost of Afghar.
How do you do, Lieutenant. My name is Tintin. But how . . .

. . . how did you get here? . . . At about midday yesterday my men noticed a column of smoke on the southern horizon. I immediately thought it might be an aeroplane and sent out a patrol. They saw your tracks, found you unconscious, and brought you in.

Oh! Did they find my friend too? . . .

Here he is! . . . Come in, come in. Ahmed, bring three glasses and some drinks . . .

So the smoke was from a plane, then?
Yes, we came down with quite a bump. The machine turned over and caught fire . . .

No thank you. I never drink spirits.
No? . . . Really?
?

Er . . . er . . . no thank you, Lieutenant. I . . . don't either. I . . . I never touch spirits . . .
You don't either? . . . Well, I won't press you.

Anyway, you saved our lives all right, Lieutenant. Without you and your camel patrol we should have died of thirst.
That's why you ought to have a drink with me! . . . But never mind about that. I'd rather you told me what brings you to this forsaken land.

. . . and here is the latest news. Yesterday's severe gales caused a number of losses to shipping. The steamship TANGANYIKA sank near Vigo, but her crew were all taken off. The merchant vessel JUPITER has been driven ashore, but her crew are safe. An SOS was also picked up from the merchant-ship . . .
. . . KARABOUDJAN. Another vessel, the BENARES, went at once to the aid of the KARABOUDJAN and searched all night near the position given in the distress signal. No wreckage and no survivors were found. It must therefore be presumed that the KARABOUDJAN went down with all hands . . .
!

That's odd, don't you think?
I should say so! The KARABOUDJAN isn't a cockleshell, to sink without time to launch the boats. It's unbelievable!

That's what I think . . . Lieutenant, is there any way we could leave today? I'm anxious to get to the coast as soon as possible. I'll tell you why.
So soon?. . . Yes, it can be done. It should be enough if I send two guides with you. That area has been quite safe for a couple of months now.

Two hours later . . .

Allah protect them!

Next morning . . .

A wireless message has just come in, sir . . .
Thank you.

MOST URGENT
T.O. 1026 S.C.
Twenty Arab riders reported near Timmin proceeding to Wells of Kefheir. Stop. Dispatch patrol.

By Jupiter! . . . The Wells of Kefheir lie on the route Tintin and his friend are taking! . . .

Ahmed, send my section leaders here at once. And by the way, what did you do with the bottles which were here yesterday?
I not know, sir. I not touch bottles, sir.

Now I'll just have a good swig of this: nobody's watching me.

See! . . . Kefheir . . .

Your very good health, my friends!

CRACK

BANG
BANG
BANG

BANG
BANG
BANG
?
The Berbers!

Quick! Behind the sanddune! . . . Dismount!
BANG
BANG

BANG
And the Lieutenant said this was a safe area!
Yah! The scoundrels!

They'll pay for this! . . .
BANG
BANG
BANG

BANG
BANG

Now, let them come: I'm ready for them!
BANG

BANG
BANG

Crumbs! One of them has picked me for a target.
BANG

Aha! I've spotted him . . . Just you wait, my friend: I'll show you a thing or two!
BANG

By the beard of the Prophet! . . . I will get you this time! . . .

BANG

BANG
?

Not bad shooting, eh? . . .
BANG
BANG

So! I've managed to crawl behind them without being seen . . .
BANG

Now for the boy: he is the best shot . . .
BANG
BANG

BANG
!
WHIZZZ
CRACK

BANG
?

BANG
BANG
BANG
ZZZZ

REVENGE!
BANG

REVENGE!

REVENGE!

REVENGE!
BANG
BANG

Swine! . . . Jellyfish! . . . Tramps! . . . Troglodytes! . . . Toffee-noses! . . .
?

Captain! Stop, Captain! . . . You'll get yourself killed! . . .

Savages! . . . Aztecs! . . . Toads! . . . Carpet-sellers! . . . Iconoclasts! . . .

Some saint must watch over drunkards! . . . It's a miracle he hasn't been hit . . .

Rats! . . . Ectoplasms! . . . Freshwater swabs! . . . Bashi-bazouks! . . . Cannibals! . . . Caterpillars! . . .

Cowards! . . . Baboons! . . . Parasites! . . . Pockmarks! . . .
Great snakes! . . . He's got them on the run! . . .

. . . and if you come back you'll feel my rifle-butt! . . .

Well done, Captain! . . . Wonderful! . . .

If those savages had just waited, I'd have shown them! . . . But they ran like rabbits . . . except one who sneaked up on me from behind, the pirate . . .

!
!

Charge! . . . After them! . . . Take them prisoner! . . .
It's the Lieutenant! . . .

Then . . . then . . . it wasn't me who got rid of those savages . . . it was the Lieutenant . . . ?

We turned up at the right moment, didn't we? . . .
In the nick of time, Lieutenant. But what made you come here?

That's soon explained. This morning I received a radio warning of raiders near Kefheir. We jumped into the saddle right away . . . and here we are! . . .

And now, as soon as my men return with their prisoners we'll all ride north together, to prevent further incidents like this.

After several days' journey, Tintin and the Captain come to Bagghar, a large Moroccan port . . .

First we'll go to the harbour-master. Perhaps he can give us news of the KARABOUDJAN.
Good idea . . .

!

?

Tintin! . . . Tintin! . . . Where are you going?

Out of my way, you!

Move along there!
Move along!

Bunch of savages! Now I've lost Tintin. What's got into him, I wonder?

Careful! . . . I mustn't lose sight of him.

?
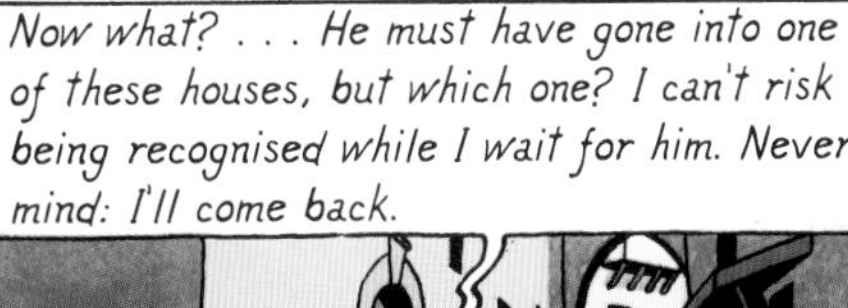
Now what? . . . He must have gone into one of these houses, but which one? I can't risk being recognised while I wait for him. Never mind: I'll come back.

How shall I ever find Tintin?

The first thing is to find the Captain. I hope he's had the sense to go straight to the harbour-master's office and wait for me there.

And now-now for the h-h-harbour-master! . . . H-h-how much, boy?
Five francs.

?

P-P-POLICE!
PO-PO-POLICE!

What's up this time?
I . . . I . . . it's disgraceful! . . . My wallet's been stolen! . . . I'll s-s-sue th-them! . . . R-r-robbers! . . . M-m-my wallet! . . .

It's dis-gr-graceful! . . . A city of p-p-pick-p-p-pockets . . . I w-w-want my wallet! . . .

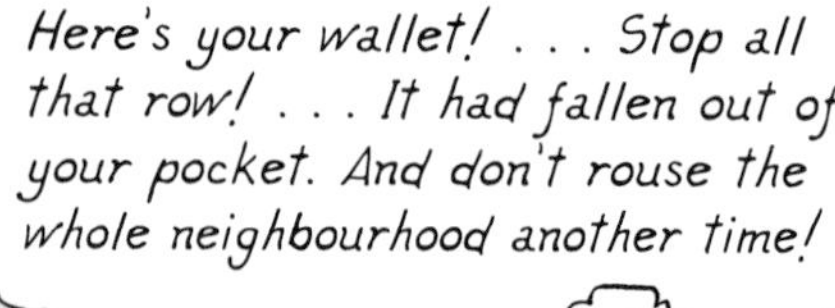
Here's your wallet! . . . Stop all that row! . . . It had fallen out of your pocket. And don't rouse the whole neighbourhood another time!

!

Now go home! . . . If you make any more trouble, we'll run you in. Understand?
OK, a-a-admiral!

Yo-ho and up she rises

DJEBEL AMILAH
?

B-b-blistering barnacles! . . . that's the K-K-KARABOUDJAN! Police! . . . Arrest them! . . . Police! . . . P-p-police!

P-P-POLICE!
PO-POLICE!

I t-t-tell you it's the KARABOUD-BOUD-BOUDJAN, Blistering barnacles! I am . . . I am her Captain! . . . It's not the DJEBEL-what's it . . . You must arrest the l-l-lot of them!
Come along! That's enough!

But I tell you that is the K-K-KARABOUDJAN! . . . and she's full of op-opium!
?

The Captain! . . . I must warn the mate at once!

HONE

Hello?. . . Yes, it's me . . . What?. . . Are you crazy? . . . You've seen the Captain! . . . Are you sure? He recognised the ship, confound it! . . . He's been arrested . . . OK, I'll come.

Meanwhile. . .
It's funny, he's not come yet. I certainly told him we'd go straight to the harbour-master.

Next morning . . .
Hello . . . Port Control here. Oh, it's you Mr Tintin . . . Captain Haddock? . . . No, we haven't seen him yet.

This is getting me worried. Something must have happened to him. I'd better go to the police.

POLI

Captain Haddock? . . . We've just let him go; he's been gone about five minutes. He was brought in last night for causing a disturbance. When he left he said he was going to the harbour-master's office and he had some very important news for you. If you hurry you'll soon catch him up.

Important news? . . . What can that be?

There he is!

The KARABOUDJAN, here! . . . That will surprise Tintin when I tell him.

Oh! My shoelace has come undone.

HELP!
H-E-L-P!

They've got the Captain!

CRASH

This wretched door won't open! . . .

The noise of an engine! . . . They must have a car!

Too late!

Another car! . . . I'll grab it: I must save the Captain at all costs!

That's got her started! . . . Off we go, full speed ahead! . . .

What's up? Why are we going backwards? . . .

?

PAAARP!
PAAARP!
PAAARP!
Stop! The car's horn must have got stuck.

?

I mustn't let them get away!

Saved! . . . There's a taxi!

Taxi! To the Central Station!
Quick, follow that car!
MB-1420

?
?

Be so good as to get out, young man: I was first.
I beg your pardon, sir, but I was before you!

My dear sir, I am not in the habit of arguing with puppies. Get out! At once! . . . I have to be at the Central Station in fifteen minutes.
And I must get to the hospital urgently . . .

. . . as I've just been bitten by this mad dog!

Quick, driver, follow that car!

Which car, sir?
Which car? . . . Why that one . . . Heavens! It's gone!

Now all I can do is find the alley where I lost the mate of the KARABOUDJAN.

But I ought to wear a burnous to go there, otherwise I might be recognised.

Ah! here's an old clothes shop . . . but . . . but surely . . . I can't be mistaken.

?
?
My old friends Thomson and Thompson.

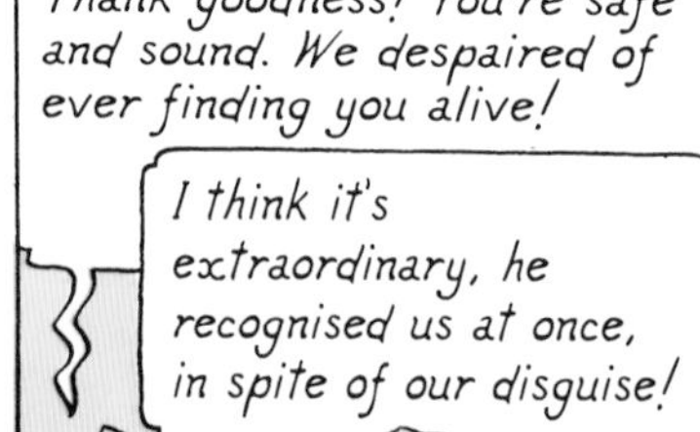

Thank goodness! You're safe and sound. We despaired of ever finding you alive!

I think it's extraordinary, he recognised us at once, in spite of our disguise!

Now tell us: what happened on the KARABOUDJAN? We were amazed when they handed us your wireless signal: 'Have been imprisoned aboard KARABOUDJAN. Am leaving vessel. Cargo includes opium. TINTIN.' We took the first plane for Bagghar . . .

. . . the KARABOUDJAN's next port of call. Then we heard about the shipwreck. Are you certain she was carrying opium?
Quite certain: the drug was hidden in tins bearing a label with a red crab on it, and the words 'EXTRA FINE CRAB'.

Tins of crab? . . . That reminds me . . .
I saw one in the shop where we bought our burnouses just now.
Did you? Quick let's go and see.

It's gone!
!
What have you done with the tin of crab that was on the table?

It's here, sidi. I put tin here in the cupboard.
That's the one! I recognise the label: it's the same.

Open that tin!

!?
There, sidi . . .

Look!
It's crab!
Of course, sidi, there is crab. Good crab, sidi, best quality . . .

Yes, it's crab all right . . . And yet I saw the same tins aboard the KARABOUDJAN, and they contained opium.
Hmm! . . . Very odd.
To be precise: very odd; in fact, very queer . . .

Tell me: where did you buy this tin?
From Mohammed Ben Ali, sidi; the shop on the corner . . .

Now for Mohammed Ben Ali.

Look!

Hmm, no one about?
To be precise: no one about . . .
These are the same tins, all right.

Hi! Anybody there!
Hi! Anybody there?

?
?
CRASH
BANG

Good gracious! Something's happened to him . . .

Thomson! . . . Thomson! . . . Where are you?

?
BANG
CRASH

???

!

All right?
Look out, there's a step.

Nothing broken?
No, all's well.
Yes, all's well.

Mind your hat! . . .

What are you doing here?
Oh! Are you the owner of this shop?

I would like the name and address of the supplier who sold you the tins of crab you have in your shop.

The tins of crab? They came from Omar Ben Salaad, sidi, the biggest trader in Bagghar. He is very rich, sidi, very very rich . . . He has a magnificent palace, with many horses and cars; he has great estates in the south; he even has a flying machine, sidi, which some people call an aeroplane . . .
Indeed! . . . Thank you very much.

Will you help me, and make discreet inquiries about this Omar Ben Salaad? . . . Among other things, try and find out the registration number of his private plane. But you must be discreet, very discreet.

My friend, you can count on us. We are the soul of discretion. 'Mum's the word', that's our motto.
Yes, that's our motto: 'Dumb's the word' . . .

Now to rescue the Captain. First I must get the right clothes . . .

Hello Mister Mate? . . . This is Tom . . . Yes, we got the Captain. He made a bit of a row but the wharves were deserted and no one heard us . . . What? You'll be along in an hour? . . . OK.

Meanwhile . . .
RUE DE L'OUE

Does Mr Omar Ben Salaad live here? . . . We'd like a word with him.

My master has just gone out, sidi. See, there he is on his donkey . . .
So that's him.

Make way! Make way for the mighty Omar Ben Salaad!
Let's follow him.

He's gone in there. Shall we follow?
Of course we follow . . .

VISITORS TO THE MOSQUE ARE ASKED TO REMOVE THEIR SHOES
?
?

One hour later . . .

How did that happen? . . .

These confounded paving stones! I tripped over.

Whew! . . . What a narrow escape!

I must risk everything and follow him. If I'm questioned, I've come to beg alms!

What do you want here? . . .
?

Alms, for the love of Allah, the Prophet will reward you . . .
Out you go, verminous beggar! Crawling worm! Begone, son of a mangy dog!
How very polite! . . .

Whew! . . . This is going to be harder than I thought. What next? But where's Snowy, I wonder?

By the beard of the Prophet! . . . Thief!
?!

Come back, you robber! Give me my joint!

Now or never! . . .
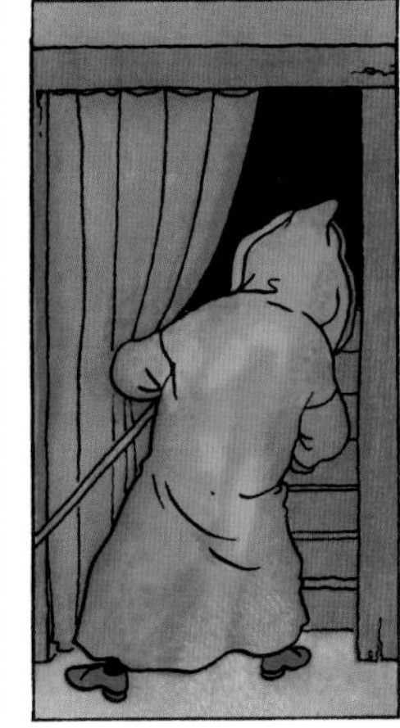

A whole joint! . . . Vile dog! If ever I see it again . . . !
Tell me, is Sidi Allan here? . . .
Crumbs! He's back already!

Yes, Abd El Drachm, he has just come.
Quick! . . . I must hide in the cellar.

Good, I'll go to him. Farewell.
Heavens! He's coming down here!

Where's he gone! . . . He can't have vanished into thin air! . . .

No secret passage, and no trap-door; the walls and floor sound absolutely solid. It must be magic.

WOOAH!

Snowy! . . . You frightened the life out of me!

You rascal, now I see. You hid in the ventilator shaft to eat that joint!

As for me, Snowy, I'm like old Diogenes, seeking a man! You've never heard of Diogenes! . . . He was a philosopher in ancient Greece, and he lived in a barrel . . .

Lived in a barrel! . . . In a barrel, Snowy! . . . Great snakes! I think I've got it!

Let's see if this barrel will open . . .

And it does! There are hinges here!

Look Snowy . . . A way out!

And a door the other end! We're certainly on the right track, Snowy . . .

Hooray! The tins of crab from the KARABOUDJAN.

BANDITS!

BRUTES!
That's the Captain's voice! . . .

Yell as loud as you like; no one can hear you. Now why not be sensible? For the last time: where is Tintin?

HERE! . . .
?

Hands up! . . . No one move! You there, untie the Captain . . .

Give me your hand, Tintin! . . . Give me your hand! . . .

My automatic!

?
Too late!

This way! Quick! . . .

BANG

What have I done? . . . Oh Columbus! . . . What . . .
It's no good moaning: what's done is done. The thing now is to get away . . .

In here . . . they're shooting at us.

?
Trapped!

We've got them! This is the only exit!

Hooray! . . . That's got them beating a retreat! . . .

BANG
BANG
BANG

?

Ooooh! All that wine! . . . What a terrible waste! . . .

Now then, no nonsense! . . . This isn't the time for drinking!
What do you take me for? A drunkard?

What's happening! . . . My head's reeling . . .

I'm the king of the castle
?
They're tight!

Ta - ra - ra - boom - de - ay
For tonight we'll merry merry be, for tonight we'll merry merry be . . .

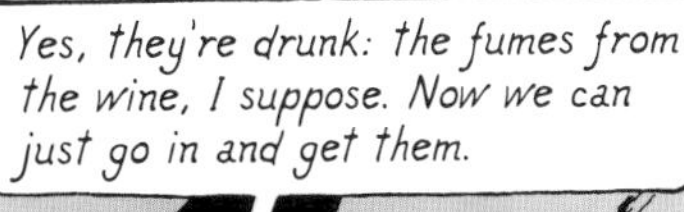
Yes, they're drunk: the fumes from the wine, I suppose. Now we can just go in and get them.

Ta - ra - ra - boom . . .
We'll take this one. You bring the other.
Tiddley - om - pom - pom . . .

I'm the king of the caaa- -aastle . . .

?
That's enough! Let go of that bottle! . . .

You bully! My bottle! . . . Treason! . . . Revenge! . . . Twister! . . . Heretic! . . . Slave-trader! . . . Technocrat!
?

Buccaneer!
Vegetarian!
Politician!
If he makes trouble I'll soon settle his hash!

Pirate! . . . Corsair!
Quiet, you drunken old fool! . . .

HARLEQUIN!
HYDROCARBON!
ABORIGINE!

POLYNESIAN!
GYROSCOPE!
?!

Revenge!

Blackamoor! . . . Anthracite! . . . Coconut! . . . Fuzzy-wuzzy! . . . Cannibal! . . .
Go on! Seek! Seek! Bite him!

Athropithecus! . . . Blackbird! . . .
Tiddley - om - pom - pom

Meanwhile . . .
See, the great Omar Ben Salaad has returned from the mosque.

Shall we go and ask him a few questions?
Good idea!

Master, two strangers are here and would speak with you. They say they are making some inquiries.
Good. Show them in; I will see them.

Mr Omar, we have been asked to carry out an investigation . . .
A discreet investigation, of course . . .
Oh? . . . And what is the object of your investigation?

A young friend of ours, called Tintin, suspects that you are concerned in drug-running.
Are you, Mr Salaad?
?!

By the beard of the Prophet! . . . Who dares suspect Omar Ben Salaad? . . . Get out, infidel dogs! Get out, or I'll have you flogged to death!

?

Nincom-
poop!

Anacoluthon! . . . Invertebrate! . . . Liquorice!

Tintin!!
?
Seek!
Seek!

So, you are Tintin! Well, this time my young friend your last hour has come!
Careful now, careful! It's dangerous to play with firearms . . .
. . .

?
BANG
!!

Who is this man?
Omar Ben Salaad! We have just questioned him, and he assured us he is absolutely innocent . . .
What a weight!

Him, innocent? . . . I've just found tins of opium in his cellar . . . And look . . .

Look at this! Two crab's claws, made of gold. He's the ringleader. I'm certain. Quick, telephone the police!

Hello, hello, police? This is Thomson and Thompson, certified detectives. After a long and dangerous investigation we have succeeded in unmasking a gang of opium smugglers . . . Yes, exactly . . . and their leader is a man by the name of Ben Salaad. We have him at your disposal.

What did you say? . . . Omar Ben Salaad?. . . Are you pulling my leg? Omar Ben Salaad, the most respected man in all Bagghar, and you've . . .

. . . caught him, yes! . . . And if that's not the truth may the heavens fall!
Quite right!

Omar Ben Salaad an opium smuggler! Well, that beats everything! But . . . what's going on now? . . .
Swine! . . . Vampire! . . .

It's him again!
Hooray! The police! . . .

Arrest that Negro! . . . He's a gangster, p-p-pirate . . . He . . . he . . . he beat me with a st-stick . . .
It's not a stick you need, it's a wallop with my truncheon!

At last, the police! . . . Gentlemen, this is the man we have brought to justice.
To be precise: . . . this is the man!

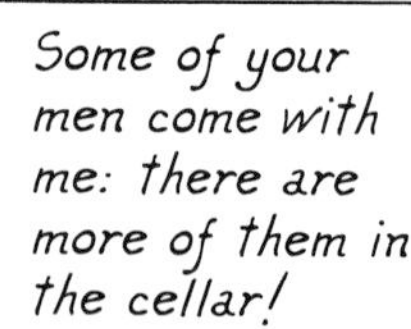
Some of your men come with me: there are more of them in the cellar!

The mate has escaped: and he's the most dangerous of the lot . . .

He must have gone out the other way! . . . If some of your men take care of the gangsters still in the cellar, we'll go after the mate.

We'll go down to the harbour. He's a sailor, so he'll probably make for there . . .

?
Police!
Police!

Someone's stolen one of the motorboats I look after! A man jumped aboard and he was gone in a flash!
There he is! It's him! Quick, another boat!

Hey, she won't go!
The painter! . . . You've forgotten to slip the painter!

Of course, we've forgotten the painter!
Wait: I've got a knife. It's quicker!

All right?
That's it!

We're overhauling him! . . . Our boat is faster than his!

By thunder! They're after me!

Confound it! . . .
The engine's stalled! . . .
Crumbs! Where are
Thomson and Thompson?

Something's fouled the
propeller . . .

A fishing net! . . .
Fine! Off we go
again . . .

Devil take him:
He's on my tail
again! ...

Take that! . . .

. . . and that! . . .

. . . and that! . . .

The boat's lurching
wildly! . . . What a fight!
. . . Ah! One of them's
getting up . . .
Who? . . .

It's Tintin! . . .
He's got the best
of it! . . . He's
swinging round,
and coming
back! . . .

Quick! Give
me that
telescope!
?!

Hooray! He's got the mate! . . . So that's the lot from the KARABOUD-JAN! . . .

Steady on, Sergeant! . . . None of that! . . . Thanks to Captain Haddock we've arrested the DJEBEL AMILAH, which is none other than the camouflaged KARABOUDJAN, and rounded up the crew . . .

Quickly!
There's someone waiting for you up there.

Heartiest congratulations, Mr Tintin!
?
Who is this chap?

Allow me to introduce myself: Bunji Kuraki of the Yokohama police force. The police have just freed me from the hold of the KARABOUDJAN where I was imprisoned. I was kidnapped just as I was bringing you a letter . . .
Oh! So it was you . . .

Yes, I wanted to warn you of the risk you were running. I was on the track of this powerful, well-organised gang, which operates even in the Far East. One night I met a sailor called Herbert Dawes . . .
. . . who was one of my crew . . .
. . . and later was drowned . . .

That's it. He was drunk, and boasted that he could get me some opium. To prove it he showed me an empty tin, which, he said, had contained the drug. I asked him to bring me a full tin the next day. But next day he did not come and I was kidnapped . . .

And they must have done away with him: but why was a bit of a label found on him, with the word KARABOUDJAN, in pencil?

Well, I asked him the name of his ship. He was so drunk I couldn't hear what he mumbled. So he wrote it on a scrap of the label, but then he put the paper in his own pocket . . .

Some days later . . .

. . . and it is thanks to the young reporter, Tintin, that the entire organisation of the Crab with the Golden Claws today find themselves behind bars.

This is the Home Service. You are about to hear a talk given by Mr Haddock, himself a sea-captain, on the subject of . . .

. . . drink, the sailor's worst enemy.
RRRING

Good-morning, Mr Tintin . . . Your letters . . . and a parcel . . .

What's in this parcel?
Why not open it?

I don't trust this! . . . It might be a bomb! Those gangsters are capable of anything . . .

To Snowy, from an admirer

Now, let's listen to the Captain . . .

. . . for the sailor's worst enemy is not the raging storm; it is not the foaming wave . . .

. . . which pounds upon the bridge sweeping all before it; it is not the treacherous reef lurking beneath the sea, ready to rend the keel asunder; the sailor's worst enemy is drink!

Phew! . . . How hot these studios are! . . .

GLUG GLUG GLUG......
...CRASH...
.....ZZING...............
.....BRR..
....
What's happening?

This is the Home Service. We must apologise to our listeners for this break in transmission, but Captain Haddock has been taken ill . . .
?

Hello, Broadcasting House? This is Tintin. Have you any news of Captain Haddock? I hope it's nothing serious . . .

No, nothing serious. The Captain is much better already . . . Yes . . . No . . . He was taken ill after drinking a glass of water . . .

THE END
HERGÉ